(FYEO)

For YOUR Eyes only!

JOANNE ROCKLIN

illustrations by Mark Todd

Scholastic Press

The author would like to gratefully acknowledge the expert and generous input from Richard L. Purvis, Cavity Nester Expert and Volunteer for the Audubon Society and the U.S. Fish and Wildlife Service; Brian Leonard, Co-ordinator, Wood Duck Program, the California Waterfowl Association; educator Vicki Zack; Jennifer Johnston, for her skillful English translation of Octavio Paz's "Peatón," capturing the voice of Lucy and her friends; Dan Levinson for Gabriela's poem; and Sasha Gsovski for her perfect rendering of Lucy's signature.

It is her deepest regret that she could not give thanks in person to the late Myra Cohn Livingston, esteemed poet and ever-remembered teacher.

LIBRARY OF CONGRESS CATALOGING-IN-PUBLICATION DATA
Rocklin, Joanne.
For your eyes only / Joanne Rocklin.   p.   cm.
Summary: The entries in the journals of several sixth grade students reveal much about their personal feelings, family lives, and a growing interest in poetry sparked by their new substitute teacher.

ISBN 0-590-67447-1
[1. Substitute teachers—Fiction. 2. Poetry—Fiction. 3. Schools—Fiction. 4. Diaries—Fiction.] I. Title.
PZ7.R59Dm 1996
[Fic]–dc20   95-39532   CIP   AC

10 9 8 7 6 5 4 3 2

Printed in the U.S.A.   37
First edition, April 1997

Book design by Marijka Kostiw

With
much
love,
to
Gerry,
Michael,
and
Eric

Mr. Moffat's Monday Morning Chalkboard

Monday, January 22

I'll place some poems
upon this spot,
some will rhyme
and some will

catch your eye
tickle your ear
make you laugh
or cry.

Each week
I'll wipe the chalk away,
but the words will stay
forever.

Lucy's Notebook

Tuesday, January 23

Welcome to our class, Mr. Moffat!

Can we really use these notebooks for whatever we want? You said we don't even have to show them to you, but I don't mind if you read mine. As long as it is FYEO (For YOUR Eyes Only).

I'm just guessing, but I'll bet you bought everybody's notebooks with your own funds. I know that teachers do not make a pile of money. I just want you to know that I for one truly appreciate it.

I'm sorry you have come to be our substitute teacher under such terrible circumstances! We all feel so bad about Mrs. Silverberg's broken ankle. I myself didn't know that stepping on a snail could be so slippery.

Which brings me to the reason I want you to read my notebook ASAP (as soon as possible): I have a shocking story to tell you. It is the story about what really happened last week when Mrs. Silverberg had her accident. I can't prove that Andy Cooper had anything to do with it. But even Mrs. Silverberg always says that Andy is a troublemaker. I am telling you this because I want you to know that he is rude and obnoxious with ALL teachers, not just substitutes, Mr. Moffat. (Although I don't think Mrs. Silverberg would have put up with those burping noises for as long as you did today.)

Andy does not get along with anybody.

It was last Friday morning before the bell. I was standing in the school yard with my best friend, Beatrice Ezra. Andy Cooper was sitting on the ground against the south wall. His crazy old shoelace collection was spread out in front of him. Andy collects shoelaces of famous and almost famous people. Sometimes he brings some of his collection to school in plastic bags with labels on them. He's got one from a famous fighter pilot who "happens" to be his grandfather. He's got the shoelace of a girl who was the Junior National Spelling Champ and was on Oprah Winfrey's talk show. He's got the shoelace of Maxie the Nose, who was almost the Heavyweight Boxing Champion of the World. He also says he's got the Governor of California's and the President's, which never leave his house. Everybody knows he's lying.

So here is what happened.

Jeffrey Fong and Todd Baumgarten went up to him.

Jeffrey, pointing to one of the bags: "Whose is that?"

Andy: "Can't you READ?"

Jeffrey leaned over to read the label. "Michael Jordan. That's MICHAEL JORDAN'S shoelace?"

Andy: "Right."

Todd: "Hey, what proof do you have?"

Andy: "He put his initials on it."

Todd grabbed the bag and looked at the shoelace. "Where? I don't see anything!"

Andy jumped up and grabbed back the bag: "You calling me a liar?"

Todd: "Yeah!"

Andy jumped up and chased Todd around the school yard. He caught Todd and pushed him down. All of us kids crowded around. Lots of kids were yelling, "FIGHT! FIGHT! FIGHT! FIGHT!"

(Mr. Moffat, Beatrice and I were not yelling. I myself hate fighting. But we were worried about Todd because Andy is very strong. He says he was trained by his stepfather, who used to be a prize-fighter.)

Mrs. Silverberg ran over to break up the fight. Andy was sitting on Todd's stomach, punching him. Mrs. Silverberg grabbed Andy's collar and pulled him off. Her nose was very pink around the nostrils. This is a sign that She Means Business. She marched Andy to the office.

Then —

I saw Mrs. Silverberg slip and fall.

4

I saw everyone crowd around her.

I saw Andy go after Jeffrey and Todd again.

Then I saw the squished snail.

Did I see a little smile on Andy's face, when Mrs. Silverberg slipped? I think so. Would Andy drop a poor little innocent snail in Mrs. Silverberg's path? That would not surprise me. Poor snail!

Oh, and poor Mrs. Silverberg!

But here you are, Mr. Moffat. I, Lucy K. Keane, officially welcome you to our sixth grade.

L. K. K.

Andy's Notebook

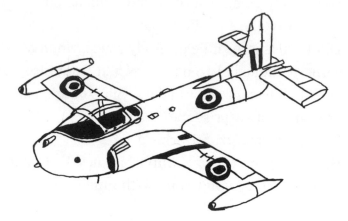

ROOTY TOOT TOOT!
ROOTY TOOT TOOT!
LET'S GET RID OF THIS SUBSTITUTE!

Mr. Moffat's Monday Morning Chalkboard

Monday, January 29

METAPHOR

Morning is
a new sheet of paper
for you to write on.

Whatever you want to say,
all day,
until night
folds it up
and files it away.

The bright words and the dark words
are gone
until dawn
and a new day
to write on.

— Eve Merriam

Lucy's Notebook

Monday, January 29

I see that you like poetry, Mr. M.

I confess that I have not read a lot of poetry on my own. Except if you count the funny poems I sometimes read to my five-year-old twin brothers, Victor and Vance, at bedtime. My mother says that's why they get so excited and jump on their beds. This is NOT true. I mean they do jump on their beds, but they are always kind of rowdy. If you looked in the dictionary under "rowdy" you'd see a picture of my brothers. That's what my father always says. (He doesn't live with us anymore.)

But back to poetry. I've been looking at those pictures of poets you put up on the walls. They all seem so friendly. Except for William Shakespeare. He looks so serious. But maybe if there were cameras in those days, someone could have yelled, "Hey, smile for the camera, Bill!"

You are the first real-life poet I've ever met.

I also confess that I have not written a lot of poetry on my own. I've written pretty good haiku, but that was only for class. Mrs. Silverberg had us write kazillions of haiku — you know, five syllables in the first line, seven in the next, five in the next.

Here is my best haiku, for your private enjoyment:

Oh, Gladiola! (5)
How iridescent you are (7)
Outside my window! (5)

I like the word iridescent. Believe me, it wasn't easy finding the perfect four-syllable word. And I think gladiola is the most beautiful word in the English language. GLAD-EE-OH-LA. Saying it is just like singing. It must be a beautiful thing in real life.

I read my gladiola haiku to my mother. She said, "I don't see any gladiolas out there, Lucy."

Then she said that even though the Seaview Apartments had no flowers, there is a very handsome oak tree in the back, so why don't I write about that? I said that it seemed to me that a person could use her imagination and write about anything she likes in her own poem! And she didn't even appreciate all the chopping and cutting down you have to do when you write a haiku. My mother and I disagree on more and more things lately.

I hate to bring him up again, but I'm sure you noticed that Andy Cooper does not appreciate his new notebook. Did you see how he scribbled fighter planes all over its cover? You've probably guessed that Andy is one of the two major banes of my existence. (My mother is the other one.) He lives in my building and his bedroom window faces mine. And he's a big snoop.

It looks like Andy is turning into a major bane of your existence, too. He shouldn't pick fights with you. Maybe you should send him to the office like Mrs. Silverberg did so we can all get some peace.

I vow that today was the VERY LAST TIME I, Lucy K. Keane, will waste my precious notebook space on Andy Cooper.

Oh — you asked what my middle initial stands for. Karla. But I like to use the initial because it makes my signature look real fancy, don't you think?

Lucy K. Keane

Andy's Notebook

MOFFAT THE WEIRDO

Lucy's Notebook

Tuesday, January 30

Mr. Moffat, will you be my mentor? I have always wanted one. Here are three reasons why I'm asking you:

1. I already have a mentor, but I don't really like her. She is Rose Ezra, my best friend Beatrice's older sister. We didn't even ask her to be our mentor. She just told us one day that's what she was. She gives us lots of tips about life and also about makeup and hairdos. Rose is beautiful on the outside, but not on the inside. If I meet her on the street when she's with her friends, Rose says, "Oh, hello," as if we'd just been introduced instead of neighbors all our lives. It seems to me it is important to LIKE the person who is your mentor.

2. I suppose a best friend can be a mentor. Beatrice is the nicest best friend in the world. We have zillions of things in common. We both love the color blue, MTV, and caramel-crunch ice cream. We hate smog and cauliflower. And we're both left-handed. When we write, we end up smearing ink onto our pinkies. We call ourselves the Inky Pinkies!

But there is one thing wrong with our friendship. Beatrice tells some of my private business to Maria.

I will not go into the details here. I think it is important for a mentor to keep things FYEO and FYE(ears)O.

3. Also, if I pour out my heart to a mentor when I am writing in a notebook I don't have to think about the other person interrupting me or not even listening. Sometimes when I talk to my mother, her eyes glaze over and I know I may as well be reciting the Pledge of Allegiance. Or in the middle of telling her something important she'll ask if I wore a sweater that day.

The problem is, my mom is divorced. I understand that she has a lot on her mind, with three kids and a stressful job and everything. But that makes it hard to pour out my heart to her.

I think you would be a good mentor, Mr. Moffat. I hope you will think about it.

Lucy Karla Keane

Karla L. Keane

(I'm glad you like my middle name.)

I am so glad that you're my mentor, Mr. Moffat!

Beatrice said you said you would be her mentor, too. We had a fight about that. I called her a big copycat, which I suppose was babyish of me but I couldn't help it. I asked her if Rose was still her mentor and she said, "Of course. A person can have more than one mentor at a time. And a mentor can have more than one mentoree."

I guess I wanted to be your only mentoree, Mr. Moffat.

Beatrice also said that she is writing kazillions of poems lately. Beatrice never wrote poems before, all on her own and not for any class. Maybe I'll write some. Well, I guess that makes me a copycat, too.

I think you look like that photo of the poet Langston Hughes. You both have moustaches, tiny moles on your left cheeks, and very intelligent-looking eyes.

I just thought of a metaphor: Poets' eyes are like headlights shining on the world. Of course your eyes don't really look like a car's headlights, Mr. Moffat, but you know what I mean!

Your friend Shirley Krasnick in the photo on the wall has pretty eyes behind her glasses. I bet the white cat in the photo is the same cat that disappeared "a snowball into the snow bank" in her poem that you read us. I like Ms. Krasnick's metaphors.

I myself have never experienced snow, living in L.A. all my life. I've hardly experienced rain, lately. Here is another metaphor from me: L.A. is an old bone in the sun. I wish the drought would end, don't you?

Another thing I wish for is a cat or a dog. I've noticed from those photos that poets like to have pets nearby when they write. I suppose pets are good listeners when the poets read their poetry out loud! The sign in front of our apartment building says NO PETS. Recently I asked the manager about changing the rules. He said, "Forget it, kid."

By the way, my friends and I were wondering: Is Ms. Krasnick your girlfriend?

Lucy Keane

Thursday, February 1

I understand what you mean when you told me that you and Ms. Shirley Krasnick are just GOOD FRIENDS. I think it is great for a man and a woman to have a beautiful friendship based on things in common, like poetry.

As a matter of fact, my mother is good friends with a guy named Dylan who lives in our building.

As I told you, my mother is divorced. She has been unlucky in love. She and my father got married when they were very young. I guess my father's luck improved when he married Matilda, our stepmother. They are very much in love. My father brings her flowers every single week. They live in San Francisco in a house, not an apartment, and have lots of dinner parties. During vacations my twin brothers and I fly up to visit them.

My mother has not found another love. I'm sad for her sometimes.

But Rose says that she can tell that my mother and Dylan are falling in love with one another. I'm not sure how she knows that. They do have a lot in common. They both love halibut and gin rummy and hockey games. That's not very romantic, but I guess it's a start. They also call each other Dyl and Phyl. (My mother's name is Phyllis.) Rose says that's a kind of sweet talk. I'm not so sure.

Rose says that Dylan would propose marriage more quickly if my mother would make romantic dinners for him. And she says my mother should spruce herself up with makeup and use a miraculous freckle-fighting cream made out of avocado and garlic.

When I shared Rose's suggestions with my mother, she gave me one of her You-Must-Be-Kidding looks (eyes wide open, eyebrows up into her bangs). That really annoyed me. I was only trying to help. I think it wouldn't hurt for her to wear a bit of makeup. And I think the avocado and garlic freckle-fighting cream sounded interesting. I may even try it myself.

Actually, the idea of my mother making romantic dinners IS kind of funny. My mother hates to cook. Most of our meals come out of boxes. It's Dylan who is the gourmet cook. He is a chef in a restaurant. He brings over lots of meals in exchange for Mom preparing his tax returns. She's an accountant.

Mr. M., a conversation I had about love the other day is worrying me:

Beatrice: "Every day I start to like a boy I've hardly ever noticed before. It's strange. It's like the flu. I feel dizzy and my heart pounds and my palms sweat. Rose says those are signs of falling in love."

Maria and Wendy said they knew what she meant.

Beatrice: "Ever feel like that, Inky Pinky?"

Me: "Oh, sure."

I lied. I have never, ever felt that way.

Maybe I, too, am doomed to be unlucky in love.

A POEM BY LUCY K. KEANE

Freckles
On-my-face
Out-of-place
Speckles.

Lucy Keane

Friday, February 2

Yesterday I got dizzy and my heart pounded and my palms were sweaty. But not because of love.

Because of HATE.

I wasn't going to mention Andy again but I just can't help it. It's a good thing I warned you about the cherry gum he stuck on your seat before you sat down. He acted the same way when Mrs. Silverberg was here, starting fights and hollering out and doing weirdo things.

Here is a tip for you: Mrs. Silverberg would keep Andy after school even if it meant he would miss the bus. Andy's mother, Clarice, had to come for him FOUR TIMES this year when he was kept after school!

Andy is terrible around our apartment building, too:

1. He draws on the outside walls with markers.

2. Once I saw him stealing an Arizona license plate from a parked car. He said it was for his out-of-state license plate collection.

3. You know how the kids of the President of the USA get special respect? Well, Andy thinks he's special just because his stepfather, Frank, is manager of the Seaview Apartments. So Andy stands guard over the basketball net and punching bag in the courtyard of our building, making my brothers and me beg for a turn. "Frank told me it's only for the two of us!" he says, even though we've never seen his stepfather play one single game with him.

4. And then there was the time he knotted together the panty hose that Mrs. Shimoda had hung out to dry on her first-floor balcony. Mrs. Shimoda didn't get mad at him. I sure would have. (Mrs. Shimoda would never even hurt a fly. Or even an ant. Really! She sweeps up the ants in her kitchen with a dust mop and then shakes them free outside — still alive!)

Andy just doesn't care about anybody but himself. Sometimes his mother comes over to have coffee with my mother. Clarice always looks bone-tired and worried. They talk for hours and hours. My mother shuts the door to the kitchen, but Clarice's cigarette smoke still smells up our whole house. Do you think

Andy cares that his behavior causes his mother to smoke too much? Not a chance.

I could go on and on but I won't waste precious space.

I truly hate Andy Cooper.

Lucy K. Keane

Andy's Notebook

LUCY THE FINK

Mr. Moffat's Monday Morning Chalkboard

Monday, February 5

THE MARMALADE MAN
MAKES A DANCE TO MEND US

Tiger, Sunflowers, King of Cats,
Cow and Rabbit, mend your ways.
I the needle, you the thread —
follow me through mist and maze.

Fox and hound, go paw in paw.
Cat and rat, be best of friends.
Lamb and tiger, walk together.
Dancing starts where fighting ends.

— Nancy Willard

Andy's Notebook

ERIC:
KING OF RATS

P.J.:
KING OF APES

OSCAR:
KING OF SNAKES

JEFFREY:
KING OF
RHINOCEROSES

TODD:
KING OF
ELEPHANTS

BEATRICE:
QUEEN OF DUCKS

WENDY:
QUEEN OF SPIDERS

LUCY:
QUEEN OF
THE WHOLE ZOO

Lucy's Notebook

Monday, February 5

I didn't know writing a poem was so hard. I'm sorry, Mr. M., but mine are so STUPID I can't show them to you. If I try to make a beautiful rhyme like that poem on the chalkboard, I end up with the wrong poem. I begin with a mountain and end up with a fountain. I end up with cars when I started with stars.

Maybe it's because I don't have a haven of privacy to do my thinking in. If I lived with my father and Matilda in their big house in San Francisco, then I could have my CHOICE of havens. When I visit them, I sleep in a huge bed. It has a brass headboard and a big comforter with beautiful sunflowers on it. In L.A., I sleep on a cot in the dinette. My twin brothers took my old room five LONG years ago when they were born.

When I complained to my mother, she told me to look on the bright side:

My mother: "You have a great view! A beautiful, old oak tree and a swimming pool. Your brothers' window faces the Astroburger!"

Me: "I would rather have four walls and a door."

So here I am in the bathroom. As you know, the

bathroom is not the perfect haven, especially when twin brothers bang on the door to let them in or to get you out to read them a story. (They are doing that this very minute.)

Me: "Cut that out!"

Victor: "You've been in there one hundred and twenty-eleven minutes!"

Vance: "Why are you having a birthday party in there?"

Let me explain. Mr M., you said we should try unusual settings when we write. So I am writing by candlelight. I stuck some birthday candles into a container of cream cheese. Next I am going to wash my hair by candlelight. I will use Midnight Mango shampoo and pretend I am in a tropical rain forest. Except it will have to be fast because we need to conserve water because of the drought.

You might be interested to know that Beatrice and I are forming a writers' support group like you and Ms. Krasnick have. We will call it the Inky Pinkies.

Me: "Mom, can you help me get the twins out of their bedroom for two teensy hours a week so I can use it for my writers' support group?"

My mother: No answer. Except for her You-Must-Be-Nuts look. Which is the same as her You-Must-Be-Kidding look, with wider eyes.

In another apartment, down the street, Beatrice and Rose are in their bedroom.

Beatrice asks Rose: "Could you please give Lucy and me two hours of privacy each week for our writers' support group?"

Rose: "You must be kidding, snotnose."

As I told you, Rose is a beautiful but terrible person. Beatrice and I used to laugh at old baby photos of Rose. Rose's legs looked like hams, her face looked like a red balloon. And she was bald.

Rose's legs don't look like hams anymore. Her hair is three quarters of an inch below her behind, according to her. Her skin is soft and clear, and her cheeks look as if she rubs them very lightly with crushed roses. She even smells like roses (Romance of the Rose cologne). She is beautiful, but I think she should try a little harder to be beautiful inside as well as outside.

Beatrice has written fourteen poems! I am jealous of her. She won't show them to me until we find our haven of privacy. How does she do it? Mine are so awful! I keep throwing them away.

Lucy

from Beatrice's Notebook

POEM # ONE: MIKE
M: Mike is a boy I like
I: I'd like to ride my bike (with him)
K: Karen also likes Mike
E: Everybody does! He's very easy to like!

POEM # FIVE: ERIC
Eric, Eric, I like your smile
I think of you all the while.

POEM # SIX: JASON
Sitting beside me is a boy named Jason
My feelings for him could fill a water basin.

POEM # FOURTEEN: P.J.
P.J., P.J., what great socks!
My favorite pair is the pair with clocks!

Lucy's Notebook

Wednesday, February 7

Beatrice and I found a place to meet. It's not a haven exactly, but it will have to do. There is an old shed near the pool where I live, the perfect size for a clubhouse. We pushed the old rags and soda cans and broken tools into a corner and brought some lawn chairs inside. Then we hung up a sign on the door that said INKY PINKIES, A PRIVATE CLUB.

Andy kept knocking on the door, pretending he was a pizza delivery boy. Beatrice thought that was funny. I had to tell her to pretend that Andy was five years old like my brothers, Victor and Vance. If you laugh at five-year-olds, they just keep on being obnoxious.

So then Beatrice was finally about to begin reading her poems. But Andy kept popping up at the window, making bug-eye faces at us. I ran out to get some magazines and we taped some pages over the window. Finally he went away.

Were Beatrice's poems worth waiting for?

No. Her poems are DORKY. Fourteen poems about fourteen boys she likes!

I guess Beatrice could tell that I didn't like her poems.

Beatrice: "You don't like them!"

Me: "I do! It's just that I like some better than others. Number six, for instance. That's my favorite."

Beatrice: "Well, Maria likes ALL of them. So does Mr. Moffat."

Did you REALLY, Mr. M.? I suppose "water basin" gives you a good picture in your mind, just like you said poems should do. Still dorky though, I think.

Lucy

Friday, February 9

It was a HORRIBLE day, starting off with a fight with my mother. And now here I am in the detention room with Andy waiting for our mothers to come pick us up after school.

This morning I had noticed an avocado in the refrigerator. I mashed it up with some garlic and oil and smeared some on my face.

At breakfast my mother had a fit when she saw me! "What's on your face?!!" she asked.

I reminded her, calmly, about Rose's freckle-fighting formula. How you put it on and go out in the sun, and you get rid of your freckles miraculously. But my mother started hollering about Rose and her crazy ideas and how dare I waste an avocado, and on and on. She ordered me to go into the bathroom and wash off the formula that minute. Of course when I saw myself in the mirror I realized how dorky I looked. But I didn't admit that to my mother. I washed my face.

When I came out of the bathroom my mother said, in her I-Know-It-All voice: "Tell Rose that sunlight *increases* pigmentation."

And I said: "Rose knows that. But Rose said all the new freckles and the old freckles blend together until you end up with one big, beautiful tan!"

It had sounded very logical when Rose explained it. It still does, sort of. Well, my mother just put her head down on the table and burst out laughing, holding her stomach and snorting and carrying on.

I couldn't stand her laughing at me. Mean things started popping out of my mouth, Mr. Moffat. I just couldn't help it. I told her how messy she looks sometimes, especially compared to Matilda, my stepmother. And I said a couple of other things, too. I won't write it all down.

I ran out of the apartment and was feeling pretty bad when I got on the bus. Then Andy made things worse.

"P-U!" he said, from the seat behind mine.

I didn't turn around. Beatrice told me to ignore him. She said Andy was exaggerating. She said she could hardly smell the garlic at all.

"P-U! P-U!" Andy kept saying, all the way down Santa Monica Boulevard.

Finally I couldn't stand it anymore.

I jumped up and shook my fist at him. "You stop that! I'm warning you!" I yelled.

Mrs. Tuttle, the bus driver, told me to sit down and stay down.

"*You* stink, Andy Cooper!" I said, when I got back to my seat.

"*I* stink! Hah! Well, P-U, you stink, too! A poem! P-U, you stink, too!" he sang.

We turned onto the freeway. Andy kept singing. I really tried to ignore him. But then he called Beatrice and me the Stinky Inky Pinkies and that was the last straw! Beatrice does NOT smell at all, except from Romance of the Rose cologne, like her sister.

"Stinky Inky Pinkies, Dinky Inky Pinkies, Blinky Winky Stinky Inky Pinkies!" he sang.

Beatrice and I got up to complain to Mrs. Tuttle again, but she told us to return to our seats immediately.

Andy was waving his arms around like an orchestra conductor. By that time other kids on the bus were singing, too, louder and louder. "Finky Inky Pinkies! Finky Inky Pinkies! Finky Rinky Dinky Inky Pinkies!"

And that's when I dumped my can of grape soda over Andy's head.

So here I am in the detention room. This has NEVER happened to me before. Andy is very happy to sit here drawing stupid pictures. He is used to staying after school. But I am NOT. I am deeply humiliated also because I smelled of garlic all day long. I kept wishing I had wings so I could fly right out the window and just keep on going. I wished so hard I could actually feel tiny wings growing right under my shoulder blades.

And while it is on my mind I want to tell you, Mr. M. — I HATE that poem on the chalkboard called "The Marmalade Man." It makes you think that there can be happy endings when I know that is NOT SO!!! Some people like to fight more than they like to dance: There are gangs fighting on my block. There is Andy. And there are my mother and father who once won a trophy in a tango contest and still fight ALL THE TIME on the telephone.

Andy's Notebook

Here's an F-4 Phantom II getting an MIG-21.
KABOOM!!! Barrel Roll Attack!!! A-A-A-A-A!!!!!
POW!!!!! CRASH!!!! KABOOM!!!!!

And here's Maxie the Nose getting it from
The Great Sugar Ray.
POW!!!! OW!!! OOOMPH!!!

Mr. Moffat's Monday Morning Chalkboard

Monday, February 12

THE RED WHEELBARROW

so much depends
upon

a red wheel
barrow

glazed with rain
water

beside the white
chickens

— William Carlos Williams

Lucy's Notebook

Monday, February 12

Mr. M., thanks for the private meeting we had. At first I thought you would be angry because I said I hated that poem "The Marmalade Man." But was I ever surprised when you said, "Better to feel something than nothing at all."

I've thought about what you said, that all writers are hard on themselves and get frustrated. Do you call everybody in your private meetings a WRITER?

And thanks for saying you like my freckles a lot and would be sorry to see them go. That was kind of you.

I like "The Red Wheelbarrow." It is beautiful and it doesn't even rhyme.

Tuesday, February 13

I am writing this in class because I have finished the math worksheet. Mr. Moffat, I like your cool tie! It changes colors depending on the light. Is it red? Is it purple? Blue? I also liked the tie you wore on Friday, the one that had "schools" of fish on it. A pun!

I hope you enjoyed the lemon muffin I gave you today. Dylan baked some for us. I can find out the recipe for you, if you like.

Wednesday, February 14

Valentine's Day Report:

Beatrice likes P.J. and P.J. likes Beatrice but he also likes Karen. And Karen likes P.J. but also Todd. I don't know who Todd likes. But Maria likes Hector and Hector likes Maria. And Wendy likes Mike and Mike likes Wendy, Hannah, and Jessica.

And then there are my mother and Dylan.

Rose: "Dylan will propose marriage to your mother any day now."

Me: "How do you know that?"

Rose: "They both have that special gleam in their eyes."

Me: "What kind of a gleam?"

Rose: "It is hard to describe. I know it when I see it."

So I took a very close look at my mother and Dylan last night. They were playing gin rummy after supper. I couldn't really see anything special in my mother's eyes. I did notice that she had some spinach stuck in her teeth from Dylan's soufflé.

Dylan had a gleam in his eye, but only after he won the game. No sweet talk, either. Except for, "Gin, Phyl!" "Get you next time, Dyl!"

It would be nice to have Dylan as a stepfather. We would always have tasty meals. Maybe we could have dinner parties like Dad and Matilda have.

Beatrice and Maria asked me which boy I like. I said no one.

Then Maria began to shout, "ANDY! She loves ANDY!"

Well, of course I said that was RIDICULOUS.

"What about that grape soda over his head?" Beatrice asked.

"What about it?" I asked.

"That was a sign of love," she said.

They both began to jump all over the school yard yelling "LUCY LOVES ANDY!" To get them to stop I had to tell them the truth.

The truth is, I have felt my heart pound and my palms sweat in the presence of someone. I have also felt a little dizzy. I felt the same way when I won Student of the Month in third grade and had to go up on stage to pick up my certificate. I was happy and scared at the same time, and also embarrassed because my socks kept sliding down into my sneakers.

No, no. The feeling is a brand-new feeling.

Sometimes my heart does not pound and my palms do not sweat. I do not always feel dizzy. I just know that I love this person a lot.

"I have a Secret Love," I said. "But his name will stay in my heart, not on my lips."

Beatrice and Maria thought that was very romantic and didn't ask any more questions. The truth is, they would laugh if they knew the whole truth. Maybe you would laugh too, Mr. Moffat.

Thursday, February 15

Here is a poem I wrote today:

THE WHITE CLOUD

So much depends
upon

a silver-white
cloud

sharing its rain
water

with the scorched yellow
grass.

— Lucy Karla Keane

(How do you like that?! William Carlos Williams
and I have almost the same middle name!)

Saturday, February 17

Mr. M., I have been thinking about that poem
"The Red Wheelbarrow" on the chalkboard. You
said that the poet William Carlos Williams liked to
write about everyday things he saw in his life. Well,
if I ever get to see a farm and white chickens I would
be so excited I would roll in the mud with the pigs. I
would chomp on the clover with the cows. I would
jump on the giant yellow haystack in the barn and
sing at the top of my lungs!

And RAIN! Will I ever see anything glazed with
rain again? Los Angeles is so ugly without rain!

Nothing I write about would be as beautiful as
that poem because Mr. Williams is writing about
beautiful things. Believe me, you would not want to
read a poem about the Seaview Apartments. Do

you think there is even a teeny-tiny faraway view of the sea? Nosiree. And Frank, Andy's stepfather, is a terrible manager. Our pool has dead palm fronds and cigarette butts floating in it. Paint is peeling everywhere and the lock on the front gate fell off. Instead of flowers on the balconies there is laundry. And if you stand in a certain spot you can smell everyone's dinner — hamburgers and cornbread and plantains and fish and tomato sauce and curry — all mixed up together. It's not a bad smell, I guess. It just never, ever goes away.

And then there are Andy's drawings on the outside walls. He draws planes and bombs and all those explosions, just like you see on his notebook. It is eight P.M. and he is downstairs right this minute, covering up his mess with brown paint. Frank is hollering at him. He made Andy paint over it four times. Serves him right.

Andy's Notebook

THE RED NOSE

so much depends
upon

giving
Moffat

a
right hook.
POW!!! AARGH!!! OOMPH!!!

Do NOT call my stepfather again.

Mr. Moffat's Monday Morning Chalkboard

Tuesday, February 20

EXPLODING GRAVY

My mother's big green gravy boat
Once thought he was a navy boat.

I poured him over my mashed potatoes
And out swam seven swift torpedoes.

Torpedoes whizzed and whirred, and —
    WHAM!
One bumped smack into my hunk of ham

And blew up with an awful roar,
Flinging my carrots on the floor.

Exploding gravy! That's so silly!
Now all I ever eat is chili.

— X. J. Kennedy

Lucy's Notebook

Tuesday, February 20

Happy Belated Thirtieth Birthday, Mr. Moffat! Enjoy the chocolate chip muffins.

Last Friday afternoon after dismissal Beatrice and I happened to be walking by the teacher's lounge when you came out with Miss Littlejohn. We heard her say: "Congratulations, Milledge! The Big Three-Oh!"

So that's how we found out you are thirty years old. And also that your name is Milledge.

I'll bet you had a wonderful celebration party over the long weekend with all your poet friends.

Wednesday, February 21

You are making the study of weather patterns and the Santa Ana winds and desert formation very interesting.

But I can tell you enjoy teaching poetry best of all. I cannot believe how many poems you have memorized! I am trying to memorize "Casey at the Bat" like you did, but it's going pretty slowly. Only 4 out of 13 stanzas so far.

I was sorry to hear that Mrs. Silverberg's ankle needed more surgery. But I have to confess something, Mr. M. It's a relief not to have Mrs. Silverberg crabbing about the noise level all the time. You don't seem to mind it.

Take this afternoon: It really was fun to wander around the school yard wearing blindfolds. Just as you said, when you can't see anything, your other senses are exaggerated. I heard the sparrows chattering away in the sycamore tree as if they were telling stories. I felt the rough concrete of the school yard and the smooth cool window of a car. I smelled car exhaust (ugh) and asphalt. But the grass smelled like a country meadow.

Of course then Andy had to go and spoil everything, shoving and bumping into everyone. I recognized his hyena howl. Then other kids copied him. I wasn't really a part of it, Mr. M. It's just that when my toe got stamped on I couldn't help hollering out like that. All my senses were exaggerated with the blindfold on.

Anyway, Mrs. Silverberg would have made us put our heads down on our desks like babies if we had run back to the classroom all hot and sweaty and silly like we did. Then we got even sillier after you recited that funny, weird poem "Jabberwocky." And when I thought the silliness in the classroom was

45

going to burst like hot air out of a balloon, you recited MORE weird poems. The noise level was really high and you didn't even care.

Thursday, February 22

The Inky Pinkies are growing, and I am not happy about that. Beatrice said a writers' support group is not a *group* if it only has two people in it. So Maria, Gabriela, and Wendy are new members. We had our first meeting yesterday. Maria writes horror poems. Wendy writes rap poems. Gabriela does not write poetry but she is a very good listener. As you know, Gabriela never has much to say. We became friendlier this year. Her grandmother always packs HUGE sandwiches for her lunch and Gabriela often shares them with me.

We are no longer the Inky Pinkies. Our new name is The Fabulous Five. (Maria's suggestion. Yuck!) The vote was 3 to 2.

Maria said it was too damp and dark in the shed and we should meet in the game room of her condo, which has a Ping-Pong table. That's when I said ABSOLUTELY NOT. We can't change everything because of Old Bossy-Head Maria.

I saw Andy slinking along the side of the Seaview
like a crab, watching us go into the shed. Sometimes
I worry that he has something sneaky up his sleeve.

Here's a poem I wrote this afternoon:

SUNLIGHT IN L.A.

Light's too bright
Except at night.
It dries the green —
An ugly sight!
Light swallows red,
Light fades the blue,
Sky's an old pale sheet
To cover you.

— Lucy Karla Keane

Friday, February 23

My friends and I believe you did the right thing
today. It was SO peaceful in class this afternoon
without Andy Cooper.

You should know exactly what happened in the
school yard before you ran outside.

Andy was sitting against the south wall as usual with his shoelace collection spread out around him. Three boys in our class walked up to him.

"Hey, Andy, any new ones?" inquired Todd.

Andy didn't look up from his plastic bags. "Can't you READ?" he asked.

"Wow!" exclaimed Mike, leaning over to read what was written on the bag. "The Mayor's!"

"Oh, boy!" added Jeffrey. "Jennifer, Painter at the Beach."

Andy smiled. "She was painting the ocean. I bet she'll be famous one day," he predicted.

"If she was at the beach, how come she was wearing shoes and not sandals?" asked Todd.

"She just was," Andy stated.

Mike bent down to scoop up a bag. "Maxie the Nose, Almost Heavyweight Champion of the World," he read.

"My stepfather fought him," bragged Andy.

All of a sudden Todd pulled a shoelace from his pocket. He swung it in front of Andy's nose. "Well, I've got Maxie the Nose's shoelace, too!" he shouted.

Andy looked at it. "Yours is a big fake," he said.

So they began to fight again.

And that's when you ran outside and found Andy

sitting on Todd's stomach, punching him, and with blood from Todd's nose all over the place.

When you pulled Andy off to march him to the office, I saw Todd run toward the school gate, his hands still tied up with a Maxie the Nose shoelace. I saw Andy putting up his fists when you talked to him. What did you say that made him so mad?

Dylan was over with a beef stew tonight because my mom is working late. When I told him what happened he said you sounded like a teacher he once had who was wet behind the ears. I told Dylan thirty years old was not wet behind the ears. Anyway, Andy shouldn't act so weird and tell those lies.

Then I asked Dylan what had happened to his wet-behind-the-ears teacher.

Dylan: "Quit. Right after we strung him upside down from the flagpole."

Of course he was kidding, but I hope you don't quit!

And it really was peaceful in the classroom without Andy this afternoon.

But the truth is, Todd and those other boys were egging Andy on.

The truth is, I'm not sure what the truth is today.

Andy's Notebook

Friday, February 23

O.K., I will write at least three lines a day at least three days a week in this notebook in exchange for my shoelace collection. Remember, you said I can write about ANYTHING and it will be CONFIDENTIAL.

My collection is valuable so guard it with your life!

My mother works in an office all day and her boss hates personal phone calls from anyone, even teachers. So don't call her. My stepfather Frank is a prizefighter at night, and he sleeps during the day. So DON'T call him either. And you can't call my real father because he is dead. The only people you can call are my grandparents if you wanted to make a long distance call to Arizona.

This is more than three lines, so it counts for more days.

Mr. Moffat's Monday Morning Chalkboard

Monday, February 26

OLD MAN OCEAN

Old Man Ocean, how do you pound
Smooth glass rough, rough stones round?
Time and the tide and the wild waves rolling,
Night and the wind and the long gray dawn.

Old Man Ocean, what do you tell,
What do you sing in the empty shell?
Fog and the storm and the long bell tolling,
Bones in the deep and the brave men gone.

— Russell Hoban

Lucy's Notebook

Monday, February 26

Tonight my dad called from San Francisco.

Whenever I answer and it's him on the other line, he always says the same thing: "HI LUCE HOW'S SCHOOL THINGS ARE GREAT HERE HOW ARE THE BOYS?!!"

If my mother answers, they sometimes have a huge argument. My mother's voice gets louder and louder and I can hear my father shouting like a wild man at his end. I get a stomachache when they do that.

Victor and Vance are no dummies. When our parents fight, they usually do something horrible so my mother has to hang up in a hurry. Last night they started finger painting with mustard and ketchup on the kitchen floor.

Then they climbed on my cot and got it all over everything. Sorry about the mess on this page!

No privacy around here.

Wednesday, February 28

I guess if you can write poems in coffee shops,

Mr. Moffat, I can write them in my noisy apartment. And it's amazing to me that you wrote thirty-two poems in the mess hall when you were in the army. It's funny to imagine you wearing a uniform, Mr. M.!

The Fabulous Five met today. Maria read a humongously long and gory poem. We listened to forty-four killings and fifty-nine risings from the dead. Then we argued again about moving to Maria's condo. It was 3 to 2 for staying at the Seaview.

Friday, March 2

I am sitting on my cot in the dinette. The window is wide open and I am leaning on the windowsill, writing. Mom and Victor and Vance are asleep because it is after midnight. But I feel wide awake. I'm not the only one. The night is awake!

The night feels PREGNANT with possibilities! I have wanted to use the word "pregnant" in a sentence for a while, ever since I found out "pregnant" doesn't only mean "about to have a baby." It also means "full of meaning." I have every right to use the word pregnant that way. Of course, I could never say pregnant around some of the immature kids in my class who would snicker and snort and make rude remarks. But I will say pregnant to the night, right now.

There. I just said, "Oh, Night, you and I are pregnant with possibilities!" I leaned way out my window and said it to the stars. I also said, "I am the Night, pregnant with possibility," to see which sounds better. I like the first way better.

HURRAY! I have discovered the solution to my privacy problem at last! I will stay up later than everyone at the Seaview and write my poems in the privacy of the moonlight. I know

Sunday, March 4

The reason the above is cut off is because that horrible Andy Cooper was spying on me from behind his window curtains. He poked his head out and asked me what I was talking about! I said how dare you and he said he was minding his own business trying to sleep in his own bedroom and he couldn't help it if he happened to hear. (He sleeps in his dinette, too.) And then he asked what's this about *pregnant*? Before I could answer, Andy's stepfather hollered at him and Andy banged shut his window. Then Victor woke up crying and my mother came in yelling at me for waking everyone up. Andy spoils everything.

But I think I have found another haven. It is eleven A.M. and I am up on the ROOF of the Seaview. This is how I ended up here:

I went over to Dylan's for breakfast. I figure that since he is probably going to be my stepfather I might as well get to know him better. Also, he makes the best omelets. You should see his refrigerator. Most people's refrigerators have only apples, oranges, and lettuce in them. Dylan's refrigerator has mangoes, papayas, jalapeño peppers, pomegranates, asparagus, and avocados. He flipped me an omelet and stuffed it with cheese, asparagus, and tomato. Then he put some avocado slices on top of the omelet like they sometimes do in restaurants.

Dylan is a good listener. While I was gobbling up my omelet I told him my privacy problems. I also asked him for a plastic bag for my leftover avocado slices. I thought I'd give the freckle-fighting cream one more try.

Dylan gave me the bag, no questions asked, and then a WEIRD and WONDERFUL thing happened: I was thinking that the only place to go with an avocado green face was up on the Seaview roof. *At the exact same time* Dylan said, "Why don't you hang out on the roof? You'll have privacy up there."

"Mom never lets us play up there," I said.

"You're not going to play up there. You're going to write a poem."

Dylan will make a great stepfather.

So here I am, on the roof. The sky is so beautiful, like a big, blank page to write on. And here is my poem, inspired by the Sky and the Night and Dylan:

OLD LADY NIGHT

Old Lady Night, how do you sleep?
Does the noise of the city make you toss and weep?
   Sirens and shouts and wheels of cars,
   Howls of cats are my lullaby.

Old Lady Night, what do you see
What do you dream from my old oak tree?
   Planets and moons and wishes on stars
   Sun coming up in the morning sky.

— Lucy Karla Keane

I like my poem.

Andy's Notebook

Monday, February 26

Here's a Republic F-105 Thunderchief downing another MiG! A-A-A-A-A-!

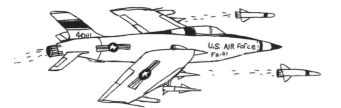

POW!!!! A-A-A-A-A-A-A-A-A!!!!! KABOOM!!!!!!

Here's a CH-46 Sea Knight going to pick up the wounded soldiers.

Tuesday, February 27

Here's a Hawkeye.

Here's two AH-1-G gunship helicopters in a search and destroy mission. BAM!!!!!!! AARGH!!!!!! A-A-A-A-A-A-A-A-A-A-A!!

Wednesday, February 28

boring boring boring boring boring boring bor ing boring boring boring boring boring boring b oring boring boring boring boring boring borin

Mr. Moffat's Monday Morning Chalkboard

Monday, March 5

MESSAGE FROM A CATERPILLAR

Don't shake this
bough.
Don't try
to wake me
now.

In this cocoon
I've work to
do.
Inside this silk
I'm changing
things.

I'm worm-like now
but in this
dark
I'm growing
wings.

— Lilian Moore

Andy's Notebook

Monday, March 5

boring boring boring boring boring boring bo
ring boring boring boring boring boring boring b
oring boring boring boring boring boring boring

Tuesday, March 6

Here's a Sikorsky HH-3 rescuing a downed
plane so the pilot won't be taken prisoner.
KAPOW!!!!!! RAT-A-TAT-TAT!!!! A-A-A-A-A-A-A!!

Wednesday, March 7

boring boring boring boring boring boring bor
ing boring BORING minus R = BOING!!!!!
BOING BOING BOING BOING BOING This is
me (BORED) hitting Todd over the head
(BOING BOING) with a salami.

Here's me with both Jeffrey
and Mr. Moffat in a head lock!
AHHHHHHHH!!!!
ONLY KIDDING!!!!!
BUT NOBODY BETTER
MESS WITH ME!!!!!!!!!!!!!!!!

Thursday, March 8

Nothing to say. Boring around here. Anyway, the
other day I was over my three line limit.

Lucy's Notebook

Monday, March 5

A few disturbing things happened, Mr. M.

The Fabulous Five were meeting in the shed. I read my poems.

"Hey, those last two are just like the chalkboard poems!" said Maria.

She was talking about my poems "The White Cloud" and "Old Lady Night."

"All you did was change the words around!" said Wendy.

Beatrice didn't say anything. But I could tell by her eyes she agreed.

In a small voice, Gabriela said, "I like them." She was just being nice.

I was so ashamed. When I heard my poems out loud I realized Maria and Wendy were right.

Then Beatrice said, "Now it's our turn. Maria and I have written some poems together."

Together! I was jealous.

"You start," said Maria. "No, you start," said Beatrice. "No, *you* start," said Maria. And then they began to laugh. Har-dee-har-har, snort, giggle, snort, holding their stomachs and practically falling off their chairs.

But Beatrice and Maria never did get to read their poems.

Suddenly the door to the shed creaked open. A tall, skinny, scary body loomed in the doorway!!!

It was Frank, Andy's stepfather.

"Shed's off-limits to kids," he said. He has an icy cold voice.

We all just stared at him.

"You heard me," he said. "Clear out. This place isn't a park! And put things back the way they were."

Nobody ever uses that shed! I'm sure Andy told him we were in it.

"Oh, who cares?" said Maria. "Let's go play Ping-Pong at my condo."

But I said I had to stay home. And here I am now, up on the roof.

There's Frank, getting into his car, carrying his gym bag. Why should he care about us using an old shed, anyway? He doesn't care about anything else at the Seaview. He hardly does any work around here at all. Clarice does most of it, climbing up ladders to fix things, lugging big garbage bags of leaves she's raked. That's why she always looks so tired. Sometimes I hear her crying when she comes over here to have coffee with my mother. Frank may be a prizefighter, but he's no prize, my mother says. And I notice he has hair in his ears.

Of course, if a person has hair in his ears that really doesn't have anything to do with the person's personality. Mr. Tepper the pharmacist has hair in his ears. And Mr. Tepper is as kind as can be, delivering our medicine in person that time we all had the flu and Mom couldn't drive.

Tuesday, March 6

Mr. M., I've been thinking about our private talk. I am glad that it is O.K. to copy in order to learn. I will try to remember your words: "You will find your own voice soon enough!"

I wonder how long that will take.

Wednesday, March 7

Today you asked me that question about diameters during math, and I just stared at you, very, very embarrassed, like a big weirdo. That has *never* happened to me before. I know all about diameters! It's just that I hadn't heard your question the first time because of my daydream.

MY DAYDREAM

I had been thinking about writing something in my very own voice.

Then I started thinking that the caterpillar poem on the chalkboard was in a caterpillar voice, small and sleepy, if a caterpillar could talk.

Then I began to think about the voice of my Secret Love.

And that's when you happened to ask me about diameters.

Thursday, March 8

I checked out those books you suggested.
I love this poem:

LIKE IT SHOULD BE

There's a blue sky I like.
I really like it.

You don't see much blue anymore.
The smog's too much.

This blue is like the books say,
Blue like they sing about,

Blue like I know it's supposed to be.

— Myra Cohn Livingston

I know that blue, too, Mr. M.

Friday, March 9

Here is a poem about my parents.
It made me sad to write it. But it is my own voice.

I WISH

I wish
your angry words
were on TV
I could turn down the sound
or pull out the plug
or just watch and wait
for the happy ending.

— Lucy Karla Keane

Andy's Notebook

Friday, March 9

You asked me what is boring. Oh, only about a million things!!!!! But I will write what I can. And draw, too. *You* asked for it! (Remember our deal: This will be way over my three-line limit so after this you won't hear from me for a long time.)

BORING IS:

1. Writing in this journal.

2-18. All the girls in the class.

19. Five minutes before the bell. Actually 300 minutes before the bell. (All day.)

20. When there's nothing on TV.

21. When you don't have a dog to walk because no pets are allowed in the apartment house I live in, although my mother said, "Maybe some day." Although my stepfather said, "No." Would like *any* kind of pet, even a tarantula.

Or a cobra.

22. Bus ride home except when you bug some-one. Especially Lucy. Her red ears look funny. Especially when she finks to Tuttle our bus driver and Tuttle doesn't do anything! And not boring when she pours grape soda over my head. I got soaked but she got in trouble. She really hates my GUTS.

23. Lucy. BO-RING. Thinks she's so great. Stuck-up. That group in the shed is dumb. Except it is not boring when I can see right in her window and she doesn't know it. I can see her right now. She sleeps in her dinette by the window, like me. Right now, her twin brothers are jumping on her bed and she's yelling. I would like to be a twin.

24. Weekends

25. Mr. Moffat's ties. Weird. Monkeys? Fish? POLKA DOTS????

26. When it doesn't rain.

27. When the Lakers lose.

28. When I have to do chores around our building.

29. Mr. Moffat's voice. Man, you sound like you need a tune-up. And you put me to sleep.

30. Writing about what's boring.

Mr. Moffat's Monday Morning Chalkboard

Monday, March 12

garbage

The stained,
Sour-scented
Bucket tips out
Hammered-gold
Orange rind,

Eggshell ivory,
Garnet coffee-
Grounds, pearl
Wand of bared
Chicken bone:

Worked back soon
To still more
Curious jewelry
Of chemical
And molecule.

— Valerie Worth

Andy's Notebook

Monday, March 12

You asked me why I like planes. I like planes because my grandfather and my father were pilots. My father's plane crashed, not in a war. But he was a good pilot. It was just an accident and I was a baby when it happened. Whenever I visit my grandparents in Arizona I get to fly a plane. My grandmother flies, too! Here we all are:

My grandfather is a hero. He was decorated in a war.

Lucy's Notebook

Monday, March 12

Can you fall in love with a poem? My heart beat
very fast when I read that poem on the chalkboard.
Garbage! I never realized that words could make
ugly things so beautiful. I noticed before that things
were more beautiful from far away. When my
brothers and I fly in an airplane to visit my father
and Matilda, Los Angeles looks like the most
beautiful city in the world. Swimming pools like blue
diamonds. Freeways like long silver ropes. But I
suppose if you look at things up close they are
beautiful, too. Even garbage.

Yesterday Dylan gave my mother a pot of fresh
parsley plants to have on hand to sprinkle in her
soup. Parsley is very good for you. I suppose if you
love someone you should think about their health.
Not very romantic, though.

We saw Frank go into his apartment with a
glorious bouquet of roses for Andy's mom, Clarice.
"Must be making up after another fight," said my
mom. Sometimes we hear Mr. and Mrs. Cooper
yelling at each other. Their voices echo in the courtyard. Love is strange.

Wednesday, March 14

I liked when you asked permission to quote from my notebook and then you told the class what I wrote about things being beautiful up close and far away and I felt like your ASSISTANT, not just your student.

Thursday, March 15

Today The Fabulous Five met at Maria's condo. The vote was 3 in favor, 2 against (me and Gabriela) to make it into a mixed group (boys and girls) for parties. Gabriela asked me if I wanted to be in a poetry group, just the two of us. She said she hadn't written any poems herself but would be glad to listen to mine. I told her I would think about it. I miss the Inky Pinkies, just me and Beatrice!

Beatrice is acting very cold to me because I won't tell her the name of my Secret Love. I was going to tell her today, but I just couldn't.

Me: "I love . . ."

Beatrice: "What?"

Me: "Nothing."

Beatrice: "You said, 'I love.'"

Me: "I love chocolate. I wish I had some right now."

Beatrice: "That is NOT what you were going to say! Nobody gets red ears right in the middle of talking about chocolate."

"I'll tell you later," I said.

"You don't HAVE to," she said. And she turned away to talk to Maria.

This is what Beatrice really meant: You HAVE to tell me if we are best friends. You DON'T have to tell me if we are not best friends.

Friday, March 16

I feel all alone tonight. I have a lot to tell you, Mr. M., but I don't feel like writing now. I will write in the morning.

Saturday, March 17

Here I am on the roof.

Mr. M., I am glad you are my mentor and I can write you what is in my heart. My mother is working late more often because it is getting closer and closer to tax time. I asked her to bring her work home but she said all her important information is on her computer at the office. She is a big grouch lately, so it's just as well. Also, she wasn't a great listener to begin with, as you know.

Last night I was invited to sleep over at Beatrice's. I was looking forward to it. Mom was working late and Mrs. Shimoda was baby-sitting for my brothers. Rose was going out on a date and Beatrice and I would have had her whole bedroom to ourselves. We were going to have a private writing group and call it the Inky Pinkies, like old times. We also planned to make caramel apples and watch movies on the movie channel and stay up as late as we wanted to.

But Beatrice invited Maria, too.

Why don't I like Maria? Is it because she has a big mouth and acts as if she knows more than everyone else? Maybe. But I am also JEALOUS of Maria because she is Beatrice's new best friend.

After dinner Beatrice, Maria, and I went into Beatrice's bedroom. There was Rose, dressing up for her date. Beatrice, Maria, and I were eating candy bars for dessert.

Rose looked us over, up and down. "Piggies, piggies! How much chocolate have you guys been eating lately? Terrible for your skin!" she said.

"Oh, Rose," said Beatrice. "Not that much and you know it."

Maria: "Lots. Chocolate toast for breakfast and

chocolate sandwiches for lunch and chocolate spaghetti for dinner."

Beatrice thought that was hilarious. Then the two of them thought of even weirder things made out of chocolate, like chocolate-coated flies and worms. They rolled around on the floor, snorting and hooting.

Rose called them babies. She had read my mind.

Later, after Rose left, Maria asked me, "Any luck with Rose's avocado freckle-fighting formula?"

Before I could answer (and the answer would have been no, as she could see for herself) Beatrice and Maria began to think of new freckle-fighting formulas for me. Formulas with mustard and mayo and jam in them. Also spaghetti sauce and prunes and soy sauce. They were laughing so hard, they were choking. And I kept looking at their nice brown skin that made them look as if they already had one big, terrific tan. Easy for them to make jokes.

Then I suggested we read some poems.

"POEMS, POEMS, POEMS. I'm tired of poems," said Beatrice.

"Let's read her the poems we wrote together!" said Maria.

So they did. Awful poems. Here they are:

POEMS BY MARIA AND BEATRICE

Lucy and TODD
Sitting on a bench
They are kissing
In Spanish and French.

Lucy and JEFFREY
Swimming in a pool
They are breaking
One hundred rules.

Lucy and P. J.
Sipping from a mug
First a kiss
And then a hug.

Lucy and her Secret Love
Swinging on the swing
First comes love
Then a HUGE diamond ring.

They kept bugging me to tell them about my Secret Love.

"NONE OF YOUR BUSINESS!" I shouted.

I ran out of the bedroom. I told Beatrice's parents I had a stomachache and went home. Mrs. Shimoda was surprised to see me. I told her about my stomachache and went to bed.

But then I got up and telephoned my father.

"Anything wrong?" he asked.

"Just want to talk," I said.

"WHAT'S NEW HOW'S SCHOOL HOW ARE THE BOYS?" he asked. I told him my brothers were fine. School was fine. I could hear music and their dog barking in the background. I was going to say more but my father said he really had to go. He had guests. "We'll have a nice, long chat when you're here over spring break," he said.

My brothers and I are flying to visit my father in just two days. But it's still pretty sad if you have to make an appointment to speak with your own father.

Then I tried to write in my notebook. It didn't feel the same, Mr. Moffat. The words were locked up inside my head because I knew you would not get to read my notebook until after spring break. If I was a real WRITER, wouldn't I be able to write anyway? I worried about that until I fell asleep.

But here I am on the roof and the words are jumping out of my head to my pen and onto the page.

There's Andy, down below. Now I can snoop on HIM for a change:

He's shooting a basket. Oops, missed!

Now he's watching a beetle walk along a Popsicle stick.

Staring into space.

Back to watching that beetle.

Staring into space. Just looked over at my window. Sorry, Snoop! You can't see me because I'm up here!

Sunday, March 18

Here is a poem I wrote yesterday.

THE VIEW FROM THE SEAVIEW

What do you hear?
my breath on the page
mourning dove on the wire
What else, far away?
groan of a bus
all the cars coming home

What do you smell?
shampoo in my hair
invisible flowers
What else, far away?
invisible smoke from a fireplace fire

What do you taste?
salt on my skin
peppermint gum
What else, far away?
a visiting breeze on my tongue

What do you feel?
the pen in my hand
What else, far away?
a promise of rain?

What do you see?
a finger and thumb
my pen, looping words

What else, far away?
a bike on a balcony
underwear drying
one boy alone
trees swaying
birds flying
over the roofs
the ocean, the sky
the world all around me
the world on my mind.

— Me

Mr. Moffat's Monday Morning Chalkboard

Monday, March 26

PEATÓN

Iba entre el gentío
por el bulevar Sebastó,
pensando en sus cosas.
El rojo lo detuvo.
Miró hacia arriba:
                    sobre
las grises azoteas, plateado
entre los pardos pájaros,
un pescado volaba.
Cambió el semáforo hacia el verde.
Se preguntó al cruzar la calle
en qué estaba pensando.

— Octavio Paz

Lucy's Notebook

Monday, March 26

Hope you had a good spring break, Mr. M.

I was really excited about visiting my dad and my stepmother. San Francisco is beautiful. And I have my own room at their house. The bed has a brass headboard and a comforter with sunflowers on it, as I told you. They have a dog named Sparky.

Well, all those things are the same, and not the same.

First of all, their dog Sparky has decided he hates me. Not only me. Victor and Vance, too. He growled every time we went near my dad.

"Poor Sparky! He's so jealous," said my father.

"Too bad for Sparky. You're our dad, too," I said.

That made my brothers laugh. But after a while it felt like we really did have this big, hairy, jealous brother with fangs.

Also, there has been an Invasion of the Sunflowers at their house. Matilda has gone sun-flower-crazy since the last time we were here. Sunflower towels, sunflower soap, sunflower curtains. Sunflower dishes, sunflower pillows, sunflower flag, waving at the front door. Dorky! And on this visit she was as strict about noise levels as

Mrs. Silverberg. When she told my brothers to stop jumping on the bed, you could just tell She Meant Business. My mom really doesn't.

"What's new? How's school?" my father asked me, just like he does on the telephone. I had kazillions of things to tell him. That's what happens when you don't see a person every day. But I left out a lot. I didn't tell him all the things I tell you, Mr. M. He and Matilda took off work to go sightseeing with us. There just didn't seem to be time for sitting down and doing a lot of talking.

I started noticing all the things that are different in my father's new house, compared to ours. Sunflowers, of course. No dust. Tinkly music playing on the stereo. Before dinner, my dad and Matilda ride stationary bikes. And they never put a milk carton or juice bottle on the table. Only pitchers. Also, I noticed that my dad and Matilda call each other Lovey and Darling.

My father seemed happy with all those new ways. He walked around with a goofy smile on his face. I know he was happy to see us. But I realized that he never had that goofy smile when he lived in L.A., with us. That made me sad. Even though I had my own haven of privacy at my father's house, I didn't mind that Victor and Vance crawled into bed with me.

But then I remembered that Dylan and my mother both like country music, and don't mind dust on the furniture, and laugh a lot together, too. I couldn't wait to get home.

I was surprised that my mom and Dylan didn't announce their engagement when they picked us up at the airport. I figured they would have had plenty of time for romantic dinners by themselves.

Tuesday, March 27

Mr. M., I guess you did not realize I have not been speaking to Beatrice and Maria when you put us together in Group D to translate the Spanish poem on the chalkboard. And I wish you hadn't put Andy in our group. But then Maria began crossing her eyes and pretending to be that man in the poem who sees a fish in the sky as he's walking down the street. Soon Beatrice and I were laughing so hard we almost forgot we were having a fight! After a while Maria became her big old bossy self, hollering, "Let's get to work, come ON!" Maria and Gabriela and Oscar helped with most of the words, but I knew more Spanish than I thought. Then we fixed up the words like a poem. The poem is weird, but cool. I, too, love when my imagination plays tricks on me, although I have never seen a fish flying among the birds.

We all liked our poem, except for Andy. He didn't help at all. He doesn't care about anything.

Group D's Translation of "Peatón"

PEDESTRIAN

He walked with the people
on Sebastó Boulevard,
thinking about his things.
Red stopped him.
He looked up:
                    above
the gray roofs, silver
beside the brown birds,
was a fish flying.
The light turned green.
He asked himself while he crossed the street
what he had been thinking.

Andy's Notebook

Wednesday, March 28

I haven't written in a long time because I lost my notebook. Well, I didn't really LOSE it. My stepfather found it over the break and read it and I got in trouble because he said it was a bunch of lies. Not the part about the planes but the part about my grandfather being a hero. That was NOT a lie because I saw his medal and this is what it looked like:

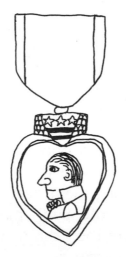

I did lie about Frank being a prizefighter even though he likes to box. I also lied about some of the shoelaces (*some* of them).

I will hide this book very well.

Thursday, March 29

Here's a Phantom II and my grandfather and me inside the cockpit.

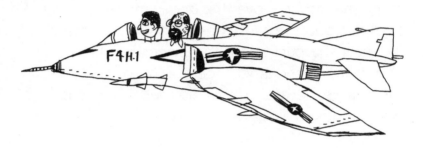

Friday, March 30

I know those planes because I got an airplane book out of the library once when I was in second grade. First I copied them from the book. Then I kept drawing them over and over again. Now I don't have to copy them. I just see them in my head. Others, too. I can draw lots of things. You name it, I can draw it.

Mr. Moffat's Monday Morning Chalkboard

Monday, April 2

PEDESTRIAN

He walked among the crowds
on the Boulevard Sebastó,
thinking about things.
A red light stopped him.
He looked up:
                          over
the gray roofs, silver
among the brown birds,
a fish flew.
The light turned green.
As he crossed the street he wondered
what he'd been thinking.

— Octavio Paz
    Translation by Eliot Weinberger

Andy's Notebook

Monday, April 2

Mr. Moffat, what I am going to tell you now is the truth:

There were DUCKS in our crummy pool today! Honest. Frank called the Fish and Game department to come and get rid of them, but nobody came yet. They glide like Lear jets, but smoother.

I am NOT lying.

Lucy's Notebook

Monday, April 2

This morning I told you about the beautiful ducks at the Seaview but now I will write down the whole story. And I will tell you some WONDERFUL information I learned tonight. I have only a few more pages in my notebook and it feels right to end my book with this glorious news! Poetry from the sky!

I saw them first on Sunday afternoon, even though Andy said *he* did. I was on the roof. I looked up over the gray roofs, just like in the Spanish poem, and there were four ducks, silently swooping across the sky. They flapped in and out between the branches of the oak tree, finally perching on a large thick branch. I held my breath and sat watching, as still as stone. Suddenly a brightly colored duck flew down to our pool. I could see its beautiful feathers of green, violet, and deep red. Another duck, a plainer brown-gray, followed. The brightly colored one skimmed the pool's surface, and did a little dance. It bobbed its head and strutted and flapped its wings. When the ducks flapped up to the tree branch again, I raced downstairs. Mom and Dylan laughed at my news. They thought I was playing an April Fool's

Day joke on them! But then they saw the ducks for themselves.

Mom immediately phoned her friend Sandy from work who is a bird expert and a member of the Audubon Society. When Mom described the ducks she was told that they are probably wood ducks. Mom said her friend sounded VERY excited. It is HIGHLY UNUSUAL and GLORIOUS that those shy birds have chosen the Seaview as a resting place. But the ducks' natural watering holes are all dried up because of the drought. What an honor that they chose our Seaview!!!

I spoke to Sandy on the phone tonight. I had lots to ask her. Here is the best thing she told me: The real name of the wood duck is *Aix Sponsa*. *Aix* is Greek and *Sponsa* is Latin. And the whole thing means "waterfowl in wedding raiment!" When I heard that I felt dizzy, my heart started pounding, and my palms began to sweat! Love is in the air!

I also found out that the flashier, more colorful ones are the males, or drakes. Mom said, "Yes, but the hen is making all the decisions about where to go and what to do next. The drakes just go along. Right, Dyl?" Dylan and my mom both found that hilarious. "Right, Phyl," Dylan said. And he put his arm around her.

I feel happy.

I have just a little room left in this notebook. I will finish it like the happy ending of a good book.

AND THEN THE DUCKS OF LOVE CAME TO THE SEAVIEW AND EVERYONE LIVED HAPPILY EVER AFTER IN LOVE AND PEACE AND HARMONY.

THE END OF MY JOURNAL
and
THE END OF THE STORY

Andy's Notebook

Tuesday, April 3

Here are the drawings you asked for. Lucy says the ducks are wood ducks. THEY are not boring. The Fish and Game people still haven't come out here to get rid of them, and I'm glad. Frank calls them every day.

I guess they're sort of like my pets.

Here are a male and a female, loafing. They do a lot of that.

Here they are flying.

Wednesday, April 4

Well, the Fish and Game people didn't come. I noticed that the ducks like to eat acorns, rice and tortillas and bread crumbs and pecans and ants. Also beetles. Some like popcorn but some do not. They all like macaroni.

Here is a male diving for food.

Lucy's Notebook

Wednesday, April 4

This is a new notebook from my mother. She noticed that I finished the one you gave me. Check out the iridescent garden on the cover!

My little brothers are writing poems, too. They asked me to listen to the poem they wrote about their favorite breakfast cereal, Choco-Bits. It went like this:

> Choco-Bits are sweet
> Very, very sweet
> They are the best cereal
> On the street!

Not bad, for five going on six. I helped them with the spelling and they wrote it down. They also drew pictures of themselves gobbling down the Choco-Bits. Then they got the idea to mail the poem to the Choco-Bits Cereal Company so that their poem could be in the TV commercial. Cute, huh?

My mother asked if she could see MY poems. I showed them to her. She took a very long time reading them. She even let the answering machine pick up when the phone rang. She liked them all very much, she said.

"Even 'I Wish'?" I asked.

"My favorite," she said.

This weekend I'm going to her office to type them up on her computer.

Last night we had a Parade of Soups at our house. Dylan brought over a French soup called bouillabaisse. You pronounce it boo-ya-baze. It had fish in it. Then along came Mrs. Shimoda with miso soup. Then along came Beatrice and her mother with chicken soup. Her mother hoped I wasn't having any more stomachaches. My mother gave me a look that said, What stomachache? That's when Beatrice and I looked at each other and smiled. We knew our big fight was over.

I kept hoping my father would call. He would hear everybody talking and laughing in the background. Then my mother could tell him *we* were having a dinner party.

Last night I kept a secret and told a lie to Beatrice. I didn't tell her about the roof, my haven of privacy. And then I lied and told her that Todd Baumgarten was my Secret Love.

By the way, I want to tell you that we thought you were a good sport about all those post-April Fool jokes. Especially the BAD HAIR DAY sign on your back. I can't even imagine Mrs. Silverberg laughing at that.

I was surprised that Andy did not play any major jokes on me. Last year he had four orders of chicken fried rice delivered to our apartment. We're pretty sure it was him.

I also want to tell you that I think Mr. Weinberger did a better job translating "Peatón" than our group did. His sounds like a poem. Anyway, I like writing poems all by myself, not in a group.

Andy's Notebook

Thursday, April 5

I worry a lot about cats getting the ducks when I'm not around.

They really look like planes when they fly. KRR-EEK!!! is their call (NOT quack) but sometimes the males go JEEEEEEE!!!! And they all go WHOO-EEK!!!! when they get scared.

Frank is getting madder, waiting for the Fish and Game people. He hates the ducks. He says they are filthy. That's not true! They take a lot of baths. You should see them flap their wings to get the water off. Then right after that, they clean each other.

Bathing

Flapping wings

Cleaning each other

Lucy's Notebook

Thursday, April 5

The ducks were splashing and making noise at 6:30 A.M. this morning. Frank our manager had an absolute FIT! I heard him down by the pool. Believe me, he is never out that early. And he was swearing: "*&^/!!!!#$$&! FILTHY DUCKS! GET OUTTA HERE!" He began swinging a broom and banging it hard against the side of the pool. Clarice ran out, yelling, "Frank, don't!" Frank just shoved her out of the way. Then Andy ran downstairs just as the squeaking ducks flapped up to the highest tree branches.

My mom went out onto our balcony. She used her polite I-Am-Trying-To-Be-Calm voice, the voice she uses whenever my brothers have a tantrum. She told Frank how excited we all were about the ducks and that they really weren't bothering anybody.

You know how a Santa Claus in a department store puts on a jolly, kind voice and you can tell he doesn't really feel that way? That's how Frank sounded: "Oh, I was just thinking about the welfare of the ducks! The chlorine in the water, you know."

But I told Frank what Sandy the duck expert had told me. She said the chlorine wouldn't harm them if they drank it. And even the water *we* drink has some chlorine in it.

"It's an educational experience for the kids," my mother said.

Frank pulled Andy over to him in a friendly way. He used his fake, Santa Claus voice again: "Good point! Ho, ho!! Educational! Andy will help me clean up the mess here."

And my brothers started jumping up and down and yelling, "Yay! We get to keep the ducks!"

As if the ducks don't have any quack in the matter. They could fly away whether we get to keep them or not. I don't even know if they'll still be there every afternoon when I go home.

Frank was pretending to be so nice, Mr. M. It's not the hair in his ears that makes him seem mean. It's his eyes, mean as a snake's. And when he let go of Andy's arm there were red marks as big as strawberries.

Friday, April 6

Today a bunch of kids got off the bus at my stop so we could all hang out at the Astroburger. Andy was walking behind us alone. He started telling everybody about the four ducks we had in our pool.

Oscar said, "He's got ducks in his pool like he's got the President's shoelace."

But I said that Andy was absolutely right. We all trooped over to the Seaview and looked in the pool.

No ducks.

Andy's eyes looked worried. I was worried, too. We both squinted up into the trees. The ducks weren't there either!

Then Todd called Andy a big liar.

"That means you're calling me a liar, too," I said. "The Seaview has ducks! Beautiful ones."

I was sure that Andy would throw Todd into the pool for calling him a liar, but that didn't happen. Andy just shrugged his shoulders. He said, "Hey, they're just ducks. They're not so great."

The whole time at the Astroburger I kept thinking about the missing ducks. I was so worried. I couldn't wait to go home and I ran all the way. I saw Andy looking out the window. I know he was watching for them, too.

Just before sunset, the ducks came back! But only two, a male and a female. There they were, perched on the oak branch this morning. And there was Andy, sweeping up duck feathers from the side of the pool. Frank was watching from the window.

"#$@$!!!!!!@$%$! FILTHY DUCKS!!!" I heard Andy say.

Mr. M., I know he didn't mean that. I saw him bring out a bowl of fresh water for them to drink.

I hope the two ducks that didn't come back have found a good home.

Andy's Notebook

Friday, April 6

I got a book from the library like you told me. I didn't think I could read a book from the Adult Section, but I can.

Here is the male showing off for the female:

And here they are in flight. They love to fly:

Over the weekend I will also draw some pictures on better paper so you can put them up on the bulletin board.

Mr. Moffat's Monday Morning Chalkboard

Monday, April 9

APRIL RAIN SONG

Let the rain kiss you.
Let the rain beat upon your head with
   silver liquid drops.
Let the rain sing you a lullaby.

The rain makes still pools on the sidewalk.
The rain makes running pools in the gutter.
The rain plays a little sleep-song on our
   roof at night —

And I love the rain.

— Langston Hughes

Lucy's Notebook

Monday, April 9

Mr. M., when I saw that poem on the blackboard today, I knew that some immature kids would make squeaky smoochy noises all day.

But love IS in the air.

Dylan brought over some ambrosia for dessert. Rose said ambrosia is a particularly romantic dessert often served on Valentine's Day. It's not Valentine's Day, but why should that matter to a man and woman in love? Rose said. According to Rose, Dylan will probably propose any minute.

Today Gabriela and I talked about poetry. She doesn't think it's silly to fall in love with a poem. When we listen to "April Rain Song" our hearts pound, and everything else. That poem is like a lullaby, or a hymn, or rain coming down. And Gabriela admitted she writes poems, too! She hasn't shown them to a single soul because she doesn't think they are any good. She just writes them down on tiny scraps of paper and hides them in an old giraffe sock puppet, which she stuffs in the back of her closet. When I was at her house, I saw the puppet. It had a very fat neck.

And Gabriela and I both love the rain, just like

Langston Hughes does. I wish it would rain!

But if it rained the way it's supposed to, we wouldn't have the wood ducks.

The wood ducks are nesting in a hole in the oak tree. That's a sure sign of love, too.

Andy drew them EXACTLY right. I didn't know he could draw so well.

Wednesday, April 11

It is raining poems in my head, Mr. Moffat.

I ASKED A DUCK

I asked a duck to stop awhile
As he was flapping by,
He landed on our poolside tile
And looked me in the eye.

"How's the water? Cold today?"
"It's fine," I answered him,
And then until he flew away
We took a little swim.

— L. K. Keane

Mr. M., here is a poem that I revised. I am doing a lot of revising, like you said you do.

SUNLIGHT IN L.A. (Revised)

The white, bright light of my city
smothers color —
red is pink and
green is dried out and
yellow is a memory.
Sometimes blue is so blue I want to
jump in,
but mostly, where the blue should be,
it's as pale as a faded sheet.

Shadows hide from this light,
Palm trees stand with office buildings
flat and thin against the sky
like pictures on a screen.
But rain will come to my city!
The white light will leave,
shadows will return,
and colors will breathe again.

— Lucy K. Keane

(I am happier with that poem now.)

Thursday, April 12

Here I am writing in class because I just finished the history test.

Very early this morning a noise woke me up. It was three A.M. I looked out the window and saw that one of the ducks was doing a dance in the water! The drake was swimming tall and straight and trying to look larger than usual. He was showing off for the hen. Both ducks were making cooing and hissing noises. Then they flew up to a branch somewhere high in the darkness.

That's when I saw Andy looking out his window, too.

On the bus this morning I mentioned I had seen him.

His face got pink. He said, "Those dumb ducks were keeping me up!"

And I said, "You can't fool me, Andy Cooper. I know you really like those ducks."

Then Andy asked, "What do you care, Inky Stinky?"

That was a very good question. Why should I care at all what weirdo Andy Cooper thinks about ANYTHING? So I said I didn't know, but I did know he cared about the ducks because I could tell by looking at his drawings. And also because I had been watching him.

And he said, "You mean you've been spying on me?" But he didn't really look angry.

And I said, "Yes. I've been spying on you. Just like you've been spying on me."

When I woke up this morning there was Andy at his window again. He said he'd been waiting for me to wake up. He told me there was an egg in the wood duck's nest! Maybe even more than one. He didn't actually see the eggs, he said. But he's been reading this book and it says that the hen plucks down from her breast after she lays eggs, to make a soft, warm nest. Andy saw the duck down. That's how he knows there are eggs underneath. The wood ducks will lay one egg a day for about twelve days, he told me.

I wonder if Andy stays up most of the night, watching those ducks.

Mr. Moffat, I think I am falling out of hate with Andy Cooper. He's not so terrible lately. Is it the ducks?

113

Andy's Notebook

Thursday, April 12

Guess what?!

The hen is making a nest in the oak tree, in a hole from a broken-off tree branch. She is using down from her breast feathers to add to the leaves and decayed stuff already there at the bottom of the hole. That's what my book says. She sleeps in the nest hole sometimes, getting ready. Wood ducks do things backwards. They sleep and loaf during the day and are up at night, looking for food.

I am not sure if they are up all night. I try to stay awake but I keep falling asleep.

But in the early morning there is a whole lot of splashing and diving and playing around. Then the silver-brown one (that is the hen) goes inside the tree. The male stands guard, protecting her, and he makes a chattering sound. That is his job.

The Fish and Game people haven't come yet. Frank told them about the nest hole. That means there are probably eggs, they said. They told Frank they wouldn't come until the eggs are hatched. So Frank is real mad, but there's NOTHING he can do about it.

I worry a lot about squirrels poking in the nest. Glad you like my drawings.

That's because I'M THE BEST!!!!!!!! I'M SUPER COOOOOOL!!!!!!!! ANDY COOPER IS MY NAME AND DRAWING IS MY GAME!!!!!!!

(I wrote a lot to make up for the days that I missed.)

Here is the drake, standing guard:

This is what I know is inside:

Mr. Moffat's Monday Morning Chalkboard

Monday, April 16

Here is an ancient Japanese haiku:

That duck, bobbing up
from the green deeps of a pond,
has seen something strange . . .

— Joso
  Translation by Harry Behn

Lucy's Notebook

Monday, April 16

What did that duck see that was strange? Was it a BODY? Was it a capsized boat? Was it a Martian? I want to know!

I am reading the chalkboard haiku over and over. It says much more than I thought seventeen syllables could say. One hundred syllables' worth!

Here's a haiku by me:

> How proud you are, Oak!
> Inside your hollowed trunk hides
> the wood ducks' treasure.

— Lucy

Our ducks probably saw a lot of strange things before Andy cleaned up all the junk in the pool with a net. Gabriela and I at the window, Frank on the balcony, the ducks in the oak tree were all watching him do the job. We heard Frank tell Andy to scrub all the tile the ducks had messed up.

Gabriela and I decided to help him. Andy got a bucket of hot water and soap and three scrubbing brushes and we got to work. After a while Andy's mother brought out some cold water and cookies and oranges on a tray. Andy put a piece of orange rind over his front teeth and cackled his hyena laugh. He made us laugh, too.

That's when Frank leaned out the window and glared at Andy. "You have a job to do, kid," he said. Frank always calls him kid, never Andy.

Then we heard Clarice say, from inside the apartment, "Leave him alone, Frank." Frank turned away from the window and we heard lots of shouting. And dishes breaking, I think.

We all got back on our hands and knees. Andy's face was pink. I wanted to throw my brush at Frank, right through that window! But Andy was embarrassed enough. Nobody said anything for a long time. Then Andy told us that Frank is always in a bad mood because he has a lot of money problems.

Well, my mom has a lot of money problems, too. My mom gets grouchy, but she never gets mean.

Wednesday, April 18

I can't wait for my mother to meet you at Open House Night, Mr. M.

I slept over at Gabriela's last night. I had a great time. Gabriela lives with her father and grandmother.

Her mother lives in Guatemala and Gabriela doesn't see her very much. Her father works night hours at a bank, putting names and numbers into computers. That's why her grandmother Josefina lives with them.

Gabriela and I have zillions of things in common. We both love pretzels, chocolate, and root beer. We detest coconut. We despise cold soups. We both love jigsaw puzzles and movies.

And we both write poems. Gabriela showed me hers. They are lovely. Some are in Spanish. I told her what you said to me, Mr. M.: "ALL WRITERS ARE HARD ON THEMSELVES." I encouraged her to show her poems to other people, and especially to you. She said she would think about it.

Another thing we have in common is that Gabriela's grandmother looks almost exactly like my grandma Anne from Seattle. They both wear big, dangling earrings and have squinty, twinkling eyes and faint gray moustaches that show up darker when they put on red lipstick. Except that Grandmother Josefina doesn't know much English. I am trying to learn more Spanish.

"¡Se parecen como hermanas!" her grandmother said.

I understood what she had said. Gabriela and I stared at each other and burst out laughing! We do *not* look like sisters! Then her grandmother said something else in Spanish that Gabriela had to translate for me. She said we both have eyes that are always looking around at the world.

Gabriela said, "Wouldn't it be fun if your mother and my father got married and you and I were *really* sisters?"

Her grandmother suddenly looked very angry and muttered something else in Spanish. Gabriela's father laughed.

"My grandmother is angry because my father is married to his work," Gabriela explained.

But I told her that was O.K., because my mother is engaged to be married to Dylan. They're not really engaged yet but it felt good to say it out loud.

Gabriela's Notebook

Thursday, April 19

Here is a poem, Mr. Moffat.

MI AMIGA

Mi amiga es muy hermosa
Su sonrisa es maravillosa.

Lucy's Notebook

Thursday, April 19

Forget every nice thing I have written about Dylan.

I HATE Dylan!!!!

Last night Mom said she had been working so long and hard we deserved a special treat. So she made a reservation at the Gardens of Taxco. When I told Rose and Beatrice, they got very excited because they said the restaurant was dark and romantic, with candles on the tables and strolling musicians who sang Spanish love songs in your ear.

Rose said, "This will be the night Dylan asks for your mother's hand in marriage. Or if he's done that already, this is the night they announce it to the world, starting with you and your brothers."

Boy, was she wrong. Again.

We were getting into the car when I asked my mom whether Dylan was going to meet us at the restaurant. She said, "Oh, Dylan won't be joining us. He has a date. Guess what? It's with Sandy, my friend the duck expert. I realized they had a lot in common so I introduced them."

Mr. M., I was stunned. I could not speak. Those ducks "in wedding raiment" were supposed to be a sign of love for Dylan and Mom, not Dylan and Someone Else!!! My mom and my brothers didn't notice how unhappy I was because the restaurant was dark (and yes, romantic). But then I couldn't hold it in anymore and I started to cry. I told my mother everything I had hoped.

My mother put her arm around me. She told me to stop worrying about her happiness. She said she was VERY happy to have Dylan as her best friend. Then she said, "I love YOU very, very much for caring."

But I still couldn't stop crying.

All of a sudden Victor piped up, "I'm going to marry Mom when I grow up!"

"Me, too!" said Vance.

That made my mother and me laugh and I felt a little better.

Friday, April 20

At breakfast today I asked my mother if my father had ever called her Lovey.

"Sure," she said. "Also Sunshine Dust, for the freckles. I liked that. And Sweetie-Poo."

Sweetie-Poo. Yuck.

Then we had a heart-to-heart talk about love.

Sometimes it IS luck, my mother said. You find someone who makes you happy, and that's that. But sometimes after a while different things in life begin to make you happy. That's bad luck or good luck. Depends on how you look at it.

I told her that Gabriela's father was a very nice man and available for dating. She just smiled.

Then at dinner tonight my mother gave me flowers. Gladiolas! They are the first flowers I've ever received.

I didn't know a gladiola looked like that. It's kind of goofy-looking with all those blossoms crowded on a big old gawky stem. But my mother and I agreed it IS beautiful, in its own way.

A HAIKU
by Lucy

Gladiola Mom,
You are beautiful because
I, Lucy, love you.

Andy's Notebook

Thursday, April 19

My stepfather Frank says he wants to meet you. He is coming to Open House Night.

I am giving you three more drawings. Put them all up on the bulletin board so my parents will see them.

Thanks for giving me back my shoelace collection. You are welcome to choose one for yourself, for keeps.

I wonder how many eggs there are in the nest.

Mr. Moffat's Monday Morning Chalkboard

Monday, April 23

POEM

I loved my friend.
He went away from me.
There's nothing more to say.
The poem ends,
Soft as it began —
I loved my friend.

— Langston Hughes

Lucy's Notebook

Monday, April 23

Mr. Moffat, I can't sleep. I am heartbroken. I knew what you were going to tell us as soon as I read the Monday Morning Chalkboard poem. I can't believe today was the very last Monday you were our teacher.

Why do you have to leave on Friday forever? I can't pour out my heart to any other mentor but you!!!!!!!!!

Tuesday, April 24

It's hard to sleep again. I keep remembering what happened tonight. Andy looked so proud, standing beside his drawings, waiting for his parents to come to school. But then I remember his face, surprised and all crumpled up when Frank tore his drawings from the bulletin board.

Mr. Moffat, how could anyone accuse you of wasting time and messing with their kid's head? How could anyone believe you are anything but *the very best teacher in the world*?

Poor Andy.

Andy's Notebook

Tuesday, April 24

The ducks have gone for good this time.

Lucy's Notebook

Thursday, April 26

PLEASE READ ASAP. PLEASE READ NOW.

Remember I told you yesterday I thought it was a squirrel or a cat who smashed the eggs and made the ducks fly away for good?

I was wrong. I know who did it. It wasn't a squirrel or a cat. Here is how I know:

Last night Andy was drawing things on the Seaview walls — bombs and jets and broken feathers. The squeaky sound of his markers woke me up. Suddenly I saw Frank tear out into the courtyard. He grabbed Andy by the neck and dragged him into the shed. I saw Andy's mother moving at the window. She didn't do anything!

But neither did I. I just crouched frozen on my cot. I started counting the loud smacks. Eight of them! They echoed in the courtyard.

Frank came out of the shed. I ducked down. He went back into the apartment.

And then my feet were running, running, downstairs and out the door to the shed.

Andy was crying hard. He kept saying it was his fault.

I asked him what was his fault. And he said, "The broken eggs."

I couldn't believe that. I just couldn't believe that Andy broke the eggs. And that's what I told him.

Andy wouldn't turn around to look at me. He kept saying it was his fault. Here are his words: "I really wanted those ducks to stay. Frank had a lot on his mind. My drawings made him mad. So it was all my fault!"

"But it was Frank who threw those eggs at the wall, right?" I asked.

That's when Andy told me, yes, Frank had done that horrible, horrible thing.

Things must be awfully mixed up at his house if he got a beating just for liking something!!! I told Andy that.

Andy made me promise not to tell what I'd seen, or what he'd told me. He said it was important. He's afraid of his stepfather. I said I couldn't promise. But then Andy said he was going to tell you, Mr. Moffat. Only you, before you left. So I promised I wouldn't tell.

But I don't know if he told you. He is too embarrassed to talk to me today, or even look at me. So that's why I'm writing you now.

Andy's Notebook

Thursday, April 26

Someone is hurting my mother and me.

Lucy's Notebook

Saturday, May 26

I haven't written for a long time. But here I am today, on the roof. I've decided to keep writing in my notebook, even though Mr. Moffat has left. That means my notebook is FMEO.

It feels so strange not to be writing to Mr. Moffat. I miss him so much.

Andy is gone, too. After that awful night when Frank beat him in the shed, Clarice came over here a few times. She and Mom had long talks. Mom told me some of what they talked about.

Andy did tell Mr. Moffat, after all. Mr. Moffat made a report about the beating. A caseworker came to speak to Andy at school and Andy asked Mr. Moffat to be there, too. Then the caseworker came to the Seaview to talk to Frank and Clarice. But Mom said the beatings didn't stop even after that. And Frank was hurting Clarice, too.

Then one day Clarice came for Andy after school. The last time I saw Andy he gave me a salute from the window of their old pickup. He was smiling. Mom said they both went to Arizona to stay with Andy's grandparents. That night we all heard Frank slamming doors and yelling, when he figured out

Clarice and Andy were gone. Soon after that, Frank left, too. He took every single thing in that apartment, even the lightbulbs. None of us knows where he went.

I thought about Andy a lot. Every time I looked at Andy's window across from mine, I thought of him. Every time I tied my shoelaces!

Then yesterday I got a letter. I was so happy when I saw it was from Andy. It wasn't really a letter, exactly. A drawing. There's an airplane flying high above the Grand Canyon. It is flying so high, the Colorado River looks like a smooth, green ribbon, far below. You can't really see the pilot but there's a great big cartoon bubble pointing at the cockpit. "How're you doing, Inky Pinky? What's new?" the bubble is saying. Swooping around the plane are wood ducks, a whole family of them. Long, skinny sunrays are touching their wings.

I taped Andy's drawing to the wall near my bed. Every time I see it, I feel like smiling. But then I feel sad, remembering how I used to hate him. All that time I was hating him, I wasn't really seeing what was there. Like when you can't see the blue sky or the mountains on a smoggy day.

Today I will write Andy back. I will tell him Mrs. Shimoda is the new manager of the Seaview. There she is now, sweeping the courtyard. She just stopped to wave at me. I will tell Andy that the twins got two big boxes of Choco-Bits cereal for sending in their poem and now they are writing poems about candy bars. I will tell him that Gabriela says hi.

Oh, yes — I will also tell Andy that Mr. Moffat sent our class a letter, in care of Mrs. Silverberg. She made copies for us. I will send Andy a copy, too. Mr. Moffat said he misses us and that he's busy with his writing and his substitute teaching. It would have been nice to receive my very own letter from him. I guess I understand.

The other day Beatrice said, "I really miss Milledge Moffat. I think about him all the time. I think I love him."

So that's when I told Beatrice that I also love Mr. Moffat, that he has been my Secret Love. And Beatrice said that Rose told her about a man who is forty-five and a woman who is twenty-five who are getting married. Rose said the age difference didn't matter that much because the man and woman had so much in common, especially bungee jumping and ballroom dancing.

I don't want to MARRY Mr. Moffat. I just love him. He is the Marmalade Man. I will love him forever.

On the day he left, Mr. Moffat gave everyone in the class a poem, a different poem for each person.

Mine was "Pied Beauty," by Gerard Manley Hopkins. I didn't really understand that poem at first, I have to admit. I just loved the music of the words: "Couple-color." "Chestnut-falls." "Fold, fallow, and plough." I loved how the rhymes turn up in funny places and how some words begin with the same letter, over and over, like a drumroll in a march.

But then this morning, the strangest thing happened. I was slowly waking up. My eyes were still closed but I could feel the sun coming through the window. I felt as if the sunlight had made everything bright and clear inside my head. Right then and there, I understood my poem from Mr. Moffat. I wanted to wake everybody up! I wanted to open my window and stick my head outside and shout, "EVERYTHING IS A POEM IF YOU SEE ITS OWN FRECKLED SELF!" But it was too early in the morning for shouting.

So I decided to go up on the roof and write in my notebook. Here I am.

Mrs. Shimoda is watering the ferns on her balcony. The cool air smells like earth and when I close my eyes, I remember rain.

Now I will write my letter to Andy.

PIED BEAUTY

Glory be to God for dappled things —
  For skies of couple-color as a brinded cow;
    For rose-moles all in stipple upon trout that
      swim;
Fresh-firecoal chestnut-falls; finches' wings;
  Landscape plotted and pieced — fold, fallow,
    and plough;
  And all trades, their gear and tackle and
    trim.

All things counter, original, spare, strange;
  Whatever is fickle, freckled (who knows how?)
    With swift, slow; sweet, sour; adazzle, dim;
He fathers-forth whose beauty is past change:
                      Praise him.

— Gerard Manley Hopkins

Acknowledgments

Grateful acknowledgment is made to the following for permission to reprint the copyrighted material below.

"April Rain Song" from *The Dream Keeper and Other Poems* by Langston Hughes. Copyright © 1932 by Alfred A. Knopf Inc. and renewed 1960 by Langston Hughes. Reprinted by permission of the publisher.

"Exploding Gravy" reprinted by permission of Curtis Brown Ltd. Copyright © 1975 by X. J. Kennedy. First appeared in *One Winter Night in August and Other Nonsense Jingles*. Published by Atheneum.

"garbage" from *All the Small Poems and Fourteen More* by Valerie Worth. Copyright © 1994 by Valerie Worth. Reprinted by permission of Farrar, Straus & Giroux, Inc.

Haiku by Joso from *Cricket Songs: Japanese haiku* translated by Harry Behn. Copyright © 1964 Harry Behn. Copyright © renewed 1992 Prescott Behn, Pamela Behn Adam, and Peter Behn. Reprinted by permission of Marian Reiner.

"Like It Should Be" from *The Malibu and Other Poems* by Myra Cohn Livingston. Copyright © 1972 Myra Cohn Livingston. Reprinted by permission of Marian Reiner.

"The Marmalade Man Makes a Dance to Mend Us" from *A Visit to William Blake's Inn*, Copyright © 1981, 1980 by Nancy Willard, reprinted by permission of Harcourt Brace & Company.

"Message from a Caterpillar" from *Little Raccoon and Poems from the Woods* by Lilian Moore. Copyright © 1975 by Lilian Moore. Reprinted by permission of Marian Reiner for the author.

"Metaphor" from *A Sky Full of Poems* by Eve Merriam. Copyright © 1964, 1970, 1973 by Eve Merriam. Reprinted by permission of Marian Reiner.

"Old Man Ocean" reprinted by permission of Harold Ober Associates Inc. Copyright © 1968 by Russell Hoban.

"Peatón" ("Pedestrian") by Octavio Paz, from *Collected Poems 1957-1987*. Copyright © 1986 by Octavio Paz and Eliot Weinburger. Reprinted by permission of New Directions Publishing Corp.

"Pedestrian" by Jennifer Johnston copyright © 1997 by Scholastic Inc. Used by permission of New Directions Publishing Corp. All rights reserved.

"Pied Beauty" by Gerard Manley Hopkins, from *The Poems of Gerard Manley Hopkins*, edited by W. H. Gardner and N H. Mackenzie, Oxford University Press.

"Poem" from *The Dream Keeper and Other Poems* by Langston Hughes. Copyright © 1932 by Alfred A. Knopf Inc. and renewed 1960 by Langston Hughes. Reprinted by permission of the publisher.

"The Red Wheelbarrow" by William Carlos Williams, from *Collected Poems: 1909-1939*, Volume I. Copyright © 1938 by New Directions Publishing Corp. Reprinted by permission of New Directions Publishing Corp.